The Kangaroo,
The Joey,
and The Cat

S. M. Barrett

There once was a baby kangaroo named Kloey. Kloey was a very sad joey. Her mother had abandoned her, and she had no one to teach her how to hop, run, walk, or do the things that little joeys do.

Kloey always cried, ate very little, and wanted to feel like she belonged. She wanted a family to call her own. So, Kloey crept into the wallaby's pen, hoping she'd blend right in.

But the mother wallaby would not (and could not) nurse Kloey, and she rejected her. Little Kloey was on her own once again, and the zookeeper returned her to her pen at the Sussex County Zoo.

But Kloey did not give up on her quest to find a family. She knew she would find one soon.

Close to the zoo was a farm owned by a nice man named Mr. Friendly. It was called the Friendly Farm. Sometimes Mr. Friendly took animals home to his farm to take care of them. People often took injured animals to the Friendly Farm because they knew Mr. Friendly would help them.

One of Mr. Friendly's neighbors, Mr. Jackson, was the zookeeper at the Sussex County Zoo. He studied animal science at college and was a zoologist.

Mr. Jackson loved caring for animals and wanted to help little Kloey.

There was a kangaroo who lived at the Friendly Farm. Her name was Camilla. She was very lonely and always wanted a little joey to take care of, but she was the only kangaroo at the farm. She seldom had any visitors besides the family's cat, Lily.

During spring break, Mr. Friendly took his children, ten-year-old Maggie and eight-year-old Noah, to the Sussex County Zoo. Mr. Jackson, the zookeeper, was happy to see his neighbors. He took Mr. Friendly, Maggie, and Noah to see little Kloey. The children immediately fell in love with her.

"You know, our Camilla has always wanted a joey," Mr. Friendly said. Then he joked, "If only we could take little Kloey home."

"Actually," said Mr. Jackson, "Kloey has been hoping for a family for a while now. Living on your farm could be great for her!"

Mr. Friendly told Mr. Jackson, "I certainly would love to, but I have to ask my wife first." Then he asked his children, "If Kloey comes to live with us, are you willing to take care of her?" Maggie and Noah nodded excitedly and promised they would take care of Kloey.

The children went home and told their mother all about little Kloey and how sick and lonely she was. They begged their parents to bring Kloey to the farm. Their mother, Mrs. Friendly, said she would consider adopting little Kloey if the children agreed to take care of her.

That night, Mr. and Mrs. Friendly decided that little Kloey would be a great addition to the farm and hoped she might help Camilla learn how to be a mother. They decided to adopt her and surprise the children.

The next day, Mr. Friendly went to Sussex County Zoo to adopt Kloey. When Mr. Friendly brought her home, Maggie and Noah were thrilled. They immediately found a little bed and blanket for her and started to feed her the special milk that the zookeeper, Mr. Jackson, gave them.

The children took care of baby Kloey before and after school, and it was not long before she was strong enough to go into the pen with Camilla. Camilla was over the moon when she met Kloey. They quickly became friends. As they played together, Kloey climbed into Camilla's pouch.

Camilla was happy to carry Kloey around.

Kloey stayed in Camilla's pouch even when she went to sleep.

The next day at the Friendly Farm, the family's cat, Lily, came running into Camilla and Kloey's pen. Camilla was excited to see Lily and tried to put her in her pouch.

But Lily did not want to go into Camilla's pouch, which made Camilla sad. She was still delighted to see Lily, though.

Kloey was upset that Camilla tried to put Lily into her pouch. It made Kloey feel unwanted, and she started to pout.

However, Camilla didn't know that Kloey felt sad, so she started playing with Lily. As Camilla pranced around like a big cat, Lily began to jump and play with her. Lily liked playing with Camilla just as much as Camilla liked playing with Lily.

Camilla enjoyed standing on her hind legs and looking down at Lily. Lily also liked to stand on her hind legs and look up at Camilla.

It looked like a perfect dance.

But Kloey was sitting sadly on the grass under the willow tree. She wanted to crawl back into Camilla's pouch, where she felt safe and cozy. Kloey thought maybe Camilla didn't want to be friends with her anymore. She didn't know what to do, so she just sat and watched while Camilla played with Lily.

It's Lily's fault that I'm not in Camilla's pouch, Kloey thought angrily.

She hoped that Lily would play with the other animals so she could have Camilla all to herself.

However, it didn't seem like Lily was ever going to leave, so Kloey began to make coughing sounds. Cough, cough. Camilla suddenly stopped playing with Lily and hopped over to find out what was wrong with Kloey. Feeling worried, she allowed Kloey to hop back into her pouch.

Lily walked over to make sure Kloey was okay.

She saw that Kloey was fine, but Camilla was done playing, so Lily left and ran to the Friendly's house.

Meanwhile, Kloey was happy to be back in Camilla's pouch, and she quickly fell asleep. As Kloey slept, Camilla made her way to a green patch and feasted on grass, flowers, and leaves.

Lily, the cat, returned from the big house after eating supper and dashed over to Camilla, who was delighted to see her and welcomed her with her trademark sound – *A-whoo, a-whoo.*

As Camilla continued to eat, Kloey woke up. She heard Lily and quickly jumped out of Camilla's pouch. She felt angry at first but then realized that Lily might be fun to play with.

Kloey smiled at Lily, and they started to play.

Camilla continued to eat.

Kloey and Lily learned a great lesson - they could both be friends with Camilla without competing for her attention, and they realized that Camilla loved them both very much.

The three of them became best friends. Camilla, Kloey, and Lily learned to live in harmony on the Friendly Farm. Kloey was happy to have finally found her family, and Camilla was never lonely again.

THE END

MS. S. M. BARRETT

As a child, long before I became a writer, I was an observer, a listener, and a lover of stories. I grew up on the island of Jamaica in a northwestern parish - Westmoreland. On long hot days and balmy nights in the town square and on verandahs, old men and women - the village elders - would tell stories. Some were true, and some were tall tales. The stories were interesting; I acquired a fondness for listening to storytelling and became proficient at retaining and retelling them.

My mother, a single parent, needed a second job just before I started elementary school. She had endured violent outbursts from one of my half-siblings and thought it would be a good idea to give me up for adoption. My existence, it appeared, was the source of this half-sibling's anger. This child had also started to become verbally and physically abusive to me. My departure, or so my mother hoped, would calm the half-sibling down and improve the family's financial situation. It would also allow me to grow up in a better environment since the "big time lady from Portland," who was to adopt me, was well-to-do and brown-skinned like me. My half-siblings were darker complected. I was my mother's "wash belly," the youngest child with a different father from the rest of my mother's children.

My mother and I waited for about a month after elementary school started, but the "big time" lady, as my mother described her, never showed up. Eventually, I registered at the local school, and my mother and I never spoke about the "adoption" again.

Before I learned to read, I would take a book from the book table and go to my favorite tree, a large Guango tree surrounded by soft tall grass. I would sit at the base of the Guango tree, camouflaged by the tree's low branches and the tall willowy grass, and I would look at the pictures in the book. At the age of fourteen, when I got paid from my first summer job, I purchased a bookcase. It is still in the house where I grew up. Under the Guango tree, I would sit and look at pictures, listen to the birds sing, eat Otaheite apples, cashews, and naseberries, and feel the wind blow on my face. To me, that was paradise.

After I learned to read, books were my escape, solace, safe place, and a getaway from the hostile reality that encompassed me as a young child. The large Guango tree with its outstretched branches was my protector, and my books were my first love. I cherished and would get lost in my books in the tall grass under the Guango tree and would sometimes stay and read until the "chickens came home to roost."

I knew then that I wanted to become a writer. For me, reading was transformative and stirred deep emotions. After successfully completing high school at Mannings, I passed my GCE examinations and completed my mandated youth service, a government requirement for high school graduates at that time. I then went off to college in America, my adopted home country.

I studied Journalism and Communications at Fairleigh Dickinson University in Teaneck, New Jersey, earned an advanced degree in Business Communications from Seton Hall University, New Jersey, and graduate degrees in both Psychology and Clinical Mental Health Counseling. A licensed professional counselor and psychotherapist, at my core, I am a writer and a storyteller.

I honed my writing skills as a features writer and editor-in-chief at a fortune five hundred company, working as a freelance writer for several newspapers and magazines in the United States, Canada, and the Caribbean. In addition, I taught English and writing classes at colleges and business schools and did pro bono writing work for churches and non-profit organizations.

I cherish teaching and giving back. As a mother, a community member, a Sunday School teacher, a foster parent to several children, a teacher, coach, and mentor to young adults, I could not think of a better way to utilize my training as a writer and a mental health professional - storytelling is my oxygen.

Ms. Barrett's website is https://www.moebarrett.com

REVIEWS

What an excellent children's book!

You deserve all the accolades for a very kid-friendly diction and an easily comprehensible body of work. It was easy to understand the theme of love, care for one another, and of course, peaceful cohabitation.

What a beautiful way to end the story - the union between Camilla, Kloey, and Lily.

Well done, and good work!!!

Ivy - Editor

Made in the USA
Columbia, SC
29 September 2022